ONLY CHILD

OTHER BOOKS BY H. M. HOOVER

Away Is a Strange Place to Be
The Bell Tree
Children of Morrow
The Dawn Palace: The Story of Medea
The Delikon
The Lost Star
Orvis
Return to Earth
The Shepherd Moon
This Time of Darkness

ONLY CHILD

H. M. HOOVER

DUTTON CHILDREN'S BOOKS

NEW YORK

Library of Congress Cataloging-in-Publication Data
Hoover, H. M.
Only child / by H. M. Hoover.—1st ed.
p. cm.
Summary: Twelve-year-old Cody discovers that the Terran Corporation, in colonizing the planet Patma, is illegally destroying the intelligent native inhabitants—giant insectlike creatures with their own language and religion.
ISBN 0-525-44865-9
[1. Science fiction.] I. Title.
PZ7.H77050n 1992 91-33037
[Fic]—dc20 CIP
AC

Published in the United States by Dutton Children's Books, a division of Penguin Books USA Inc.
375 Hudson Street, New York, New York 10014

Designer: Joseph Rutt

Printed in U.S.A. First Edition 10 9 8 7 6 5 4 3 2 1

Chapter 1

Cody was born in a spaceship named the *Annie Cannon.* He never went outside that ship until he was twelve years old. This is the story of what happened to him then.

He wasn't supposed to be on the ship. The corporation that owned the *Annie Cannon* didn't allow children on their research vessels. But Cody had been born two light-years away from Earth—too far out to turn back. As punishment for having him, both his parents had been fined a year's salary and demoted a grade in rank.

Cody had overheard that story from two crewmen. He found it interesting, but puzzling. It explained why there were no other children, but not why his parents had disobeyed orders. They weren't the type.

His father was a flight engineer named Gus Oakton. He worked on the control deck where only authorized people were allowed, so Cody didn't see him often. Gus always smiled when they met but seldom had more to say than, "Hi. How you doing?" Cody used to tell him—before he grew old enough to know the man didn't really expect an answer. Now Cody simply said, "Just fine, sir," and Gus would salute him and walk on. Cody thought Gus was boring.

His mother, Olivia Palchek, was one of the ship's doctors, a neurobiologist. She monitored the effect of cosmic radiation on the crew. When she gave Cody his monthly checkup, she would talk to him about her work. Once she explained that, in spite of the ship's deflector shields, the crew was always in danger from speeding particles coming through the hulls. "Zip! You've lost a brain cell. Too many *zips* and you're dead," she said. That idea scared him so much that he had nightmares, and Avi got mad at Dr. Palchek.

Cody respected his mother, but he loved Avi.

Avi—Dr. Emily Avichenko—was his favorite person in the whole ship. From the time he was a baby, his mother had welcomed her colleagues' help in caring for him. He grew up remembering that it was Avi who had fed and dressed him when he was little, who made a fuss when he got sick, who chased bad dreams away and made him feel safe again.

Cody thought of his parents as Gus and Olivia, not as *Father* and *Mother.* They weren't that special to him. He didn't feel deprived. With no other children or parents to compare things to, he saw nothing wrong with his life.

He had a lot of friends among the crew. All his playmates were highly educated adults. He had his own room in the medical officer's quarters. His uniforms and boots were custom-made by the supply officer. The machinists and robotics technicians made him wonderful toys. His lessons were designed by the ship's historian and two of the data experts. People taught him all sorts of things, from sports and dancing to their scientific specialty.

All this was normal to him. What seemed strange was the idea of life outside the ship.

Then one morning at breakfast, a major announcement came over the intercom. The ship's commander said they were fast approaching an

Earth-type planet named Patma. Once the ship reached orbit, the entire crew would be given leave. While a maintenance team came aboard to work on the *Annie Cannon,* her crew could spend at least a month vacationing on the planet's surface.

"That includes you, Cody," the commander said, and everybody in the dining room applauded. "You'll be the youngest person ever to walk on that world."

Cody was very excited. He could remember when the ship orbited two other planets. He had never been allowed to visit either surface with the science crews—no matter how often he asked. "Too dangerous for a kid," the commander had always said.

Gulping down his breakfast, Cody hurried off to his computer to learn all he could about this new planet.

A picture of Patma came on-screen. It showed a huge green, white, and tan ball turning in black space, orbited by three moons—one dirty white, one rusty, and one gray.

The computer said the Terran Corporation had discovered and claimed Patma some three hundred Earth years before. The atmosphere was viable; the planet's size and gravity were slightly greater than Earth's. Water covered half the surface. The small southern continent was cold and desertlike. The two big northern continents were forest and grassland.

After the planet had been charted and explored, the computer said, "Commercial development made Patma famous for the export of its exotic gems, hardwoods, and exquisitely bizarre seashells." Pictures were shown of these items.

During the next few days, Avi and the others told him more. Patma was so far from Earth's solar system, they said, that it was a real frontier world. The only law was corporate law. The law was enforced mainly in Patma City, the only real town. If you left the town, you had to be careful.

No one was allowed to move to Patma unless they worked for the corporation. Many of those who came were social misfits, attracted by the isolation or the hardship wages or both. Mining and lumber experts came for specific duty tours. Tourists with lots of time and money stopped off on world cruises.

There were two hotels in Patma City. The corporation used the planet as a rest-and-recreation stop for the crews of its many ships.

Cody's friends also tried to tell him how it felt to walk on a planet's surface, to be out in the open. He tried to imagine it but couldn't, although he could hardly wait to find out. He was packed and ready two days before the *Annie Cannon* reached orbit. Transport put him on the third shuttle.

His first ride in a shuttle craft was thrilling but scary. Being weightless was fun. Strapped into the recliner cradle, he laughed when his arms and legs tried to float toward the ceiling. Soon, however, his stomach felt as if it wanted to float, too. In spite of the drug he'd been given, he got space-sick and threw up into a plastic bag.

Having gravity return was worse. As the shuttle entered Patma's atmosphere, G-force increased until he was sure he was going to be pushed right through the back of the recliner. His face hurt as gravity forced his lips back into a ghastly smile.

By final orbit, the shuttle had slowed. On the screen in front of the cabin, he saw a flash-by view of ocean and then the port, a gray expanse of pavement flanked by warehouses. Beyond, set back from the beach, were clusters of low buildings half-hidden by greenery.

"That's Patma City," Avi told him.

The shuttle glided over the town and landed on a cape a few miles away. This was the corporate crew compound. It contained a hotel, offices, and a medical center.

When the shuttle hatch opened, Cody waited impatiently until it was his turn to get off. He gave an excited yell and ran down the ramp into the sunshine, then slowed . . . and stopped. People dodged around him.

He was used to walls and ceilings. Out here there was *nothing* to protect him. This place was so big that he could see . . . forever! Overhead was the sky, an endless pale blue emptiness. He'd never seen true sky—only black, star-misted space framed by a screen. The ship had no windows.

He knew the bright sun up there was the star this planet orbited. Stars emitted the killer particles that Olivia had warned him about. He'd never been so close to a star. Its reflected heat rose up from the pavement, warming his bare arms and legs.

With the heat came new smells—dust and hot metal from the cooling shuttle, the ocean's heavy odor, and a mixture of rich scents from plants and soil.

As the strangeness of the place flooded in on him, he began to feel dizzy. His knees went weak and wobbly, and he grabbed hold of the railing. Then, without knowing why, he crouched down, totally terrified.

Just then he saw Olivia. She was standing off

to one side of the ramp, recording his humiliation with a camcorder.

Only pride kept him from running back into the shuttle and begging the pilot to return him to the ship at once.

Chapter 2

"Scary, isn't it?" Avi caught up with him on the ramp, put her hand under his arm, and pulled him up. "All this open space. For the first few days off the ship, I always want to hide in a closet."

"It scares *you,* too?" Cody managed to walk with her down the ramp, but his legs felt weak.

"It scares everybody. Some just won't admit it. Why do you think some people volunteered to stay aboard and help clean the ship?"

"They were scared?"

"Yes."

He felt better hearing that and took a deep breath of the strange, warm air. "Do you get over being scared?"

"Yes," Avi assured him. "You'll see. By the time we leave, you'll wonder how you can stand being shut up in the ship again for months." She grinned down at him. "Come on, let's take a walk. It will help us get used to being here."

As they toured the grounds, Cody decided the hotel was nice. Tall treelike plants shaded flat green areas called lawns. There were lots of flowers. The ship had a small swimming pool. This place had two pools, both huge, as were the game courts. There was a fleet of air cars for rent. He'd never seen a real air car and spent so much time looking at them that Avi got bored.

He was surprised to see a rack of bicycles just like the ones they rode to get around the ship. It hadn't occurred to him that bikes could be ridden on land.

A warm breeze blew, making the trees sway. Wind was a new thing and slightly alarming to a boy who had never felt more than a mild draft. He thought it was interesting that wind made sounds and carried smells. There were many strange noises. Avi said, "They're made by insects and birds—not Earth-type birds, but we call them that."

The ocean was awesome. He could hardly believe there could be that much water anywhere. And it was *green.* He'd never known water had color. One of the tapes he'd studied about Patma said ocean water was treated for human use. He wondered how they filtered out the color.

"The hotel looks like a circle of giant cupcakes with windows and all different colored icing," he told Avi as they walked back across the lawn from the beach. "How many people does it hold?"

"About three thousand. It can accommodate three crews. Plus the hotel staff."

Two of those crews would be strangers, he thought to himself. He had never met a stranger.

They entered the hotel. He saw that each round building contained a circular lounge. On each floor, doors off the lounge opened into wedge-shaped rooms, each with its own sanit and the luxury of a bathtub. The furnishings were simple. Green carpet and blue bedding—the corporate colors—gave the rooms a cool and restful look.

Cody was in G-3, on the ground floor. Avi was next door. He liked his room, except that almost one whole wall was window and overlooked the ocean. The first thing he did was close the window panel to shut out the view. Then, feeling safer, he sat down on the bed and bounced a few times to check it out. The bed was bigger and softer than his bed at home on the ship.

His luggage had arrived and was just inside the door. His computer, still closed, was on the table by the window. Deciding that the table was meant to be his desk, he frowned. Everyone got a vacation but him. He had to keep up with his lessons.

From the lounge outside came familiar voices as more of the crew arrived. They sounded in a party mood, all except one angry voice.

"Was that what you intended? To do a study on him? This is a long-term experiment for you?"

It took a few seconds for Cody to realize the angry voice was Avi's. He jumped up to see what was going on.

To his surprise, Avi was talking to his mother. When Dr. Palchek saw her son looking at them, she turned and walked away, tucking her camcorder into her pocket as she went. Avi glanced around and saw him, then followed Dr. Palchek out of the lounge.

Curious, Cody slowly walked over to where his mother had been standing. From there, he had a clear view of his own bed. Seeing that, he blushed, remembering her camcorder aimed at him when he panicked on the shuttle ramp. She must have been filming him in his room, too. Why? And why would it make Avi so angry? What sort of study could Olivia do on him?

"Hey, Little Bit, what's the problem?" Emory, one of the geologists, paused on his way to the elevator. He carried a bulging duffel bag on his shoulder. A rock hammer and power chisels hung from his belt. He was thirty years old, the youngest man on the ship, next to Cody. "You forget your room number?"

". . . no."

Emory was from a wonderful place called Tennessee—which he never tired of telling Cody about. Cody liked him a lot but wished he would stop calling him that stupid name, *Little Bit*.

"Why you standing there looking down-in-the-mouth, boy?"

"I'm thinking."

"Don't do that!" Laughing, Emory shrugged to shift the heavy bag on his shoulder. "We all live too close together to think. Especially about things that make us frown. Whatever it is, let it be." He shrugged again. "Just let me get settled in here, and then I'll show you how to fly an air scooter. That's the fun of being on a planet—it's the only place you really get to fly in space. You'll like it!"

When he saw Avi at lunchtime, Cody asked, "Why is Olivia following me around with her camcorder?"

Avi hesitated before answering. "You're her son. She wants a record of your visit here."

Cody knew his friend better than that. "Why would that make you so mad?"

"She's interested in your . . . reactions to the planet."

"Because I'm scared?"

"Not just that—"

"Will she show that film to people?"

"Probably not."

"How do you know? You said she was studying me."

"Cody, your situation is unique. You're a child. You've never been on a planet. As a neurobiologist, she wants to see how it affects you, physically and mentally. You know we all have to get physicals when we get back to the ship. It's part of that, just a little more so for you. Don't worry about it."

Because he sensed Avi wanted him to drop

the subject, Cody did, but he didn't forget about it. "I'll show Olivia," he vowed to himself. "I won't be afraid, no matter what happens. And even if I am, I won't let it show."

He went back to his room, opened the window panel, and made himself look out. When he got up enough courage, he went out into the courtyard. The fountain jetted water in the shape of a big round ball. Rainbows danced above the spray. The covered walkways connecting the buildings were edged with red flowers.

He sniffed. Mint. The smell came from the ground. Squatting down he discovered the smell came from the flowers, which was interesting. Flowers grown in the ship's greenpods had no scent. Maybe because they were a different kind.

A scuff of gravel made him look up. There was his mother, putting her camcorder in her pocket again. She gave him a guilty smile. "The flowers are lovely, aren't they?"

"What are you going to do with that?" Cody said, ignoring her question. "Show people how scared I was?"

"Of course not. Don't be hostile, Cody. Part of my records will go into your bio-file." She paused. "And I'll give you a copy. I thought perhaps . . . in time . . . you might appreciate seeing this. As a memento. Photography is, uh, a minor hobby of mine." She gave him a tentative smile. "You might enjoy it, too. Have you ever tried it?"

"I don't have a camcorder." Cody was diverted from his original question—as his mother had intended.

"I'll get you one," said Dr. Palchek.

"Thank you, but Avi doesn't like it when people give me expensive gifts. She says they spoil me."

"She won't accuse me of that," Dr. Palchek said and walked away. Cody wasn't sure what she meant.

"I told you, boy, there's no time for frowns" was Emory's greeting as he came into the courtyard. "We've got to go make a pilot out of you. Right now. No time to lose."

Cody had to remind himself not to be afraid as Emory led the way through a maze of shrubbery, past the swimming pools, and out beyond all the buildings. There, shaded by a roof on poles, were ten of what looked like a round metal cage with a seat inside. Each stood on a flat metal box. A small control panel faced the seat.

"Air scooters," said Emory. "Antigrav lifts. The cage serves as a rollbar if you land wrong. Knowing how fast you learn, you won't have many problems."

He reached into the nearest cage and touched a white spot on the control panel. The unit floated up a few inches. As it hovered, Emory tipped it sideways so Cody could see underneath. There was a box with pipes coming out of it and several metal fins.

"They'll go up about ten feet with my weight, maybe twice that high with yours," Emory said. "Here's the drive cell. These are control buttons. Green is up, brown down, red is right, blue left. Watch me."

Pulling the scooter back to the ground, Emory slid inside. As the seatbelt closed, the round cage lifted and quickly backed away from Cody. Emory touched the blue spot and flew in a circle, calling, "See how easy?" He flew a fancy figure eight. "Now you fly that one," he said, pointing.

Five minutes later, Cody had learned enough of the basics to follow his friend over the lawn and out across a brown field splashed with brilliant white and yellow flowers.

The next hour was the best time Cody had ever had in his life. The freedom of flying was wonderful. No one had thought to tell him how beautiful planets could be. There were flowers and birds, all bright colors. On the ground, animals ran when the shadows of the scooters passed over them. In the distance the ocean sparkled with silver and gold. Every few minutes he wished he had a camcorder so he could always remember this just as it happened.

By the time Emory said they had to go back, Cody was over his fear of open spaces.

His mother was true to her word. The next morning Cody nearly stumbled over a package left outside his door. In it was a camcorder twice the size of hers and, to Cody's eyes, twice as nice.

The recorded instructions built into the camcorder said it would ". . . faithfully record anything within range of lens and microphone."

To his surprise Avi didn't object to this gift. She even seemed pleased that Olivia had given it to him. "That's very thoughtful of her," Avi said. "You should have one. I'm sorry I didn't think of it myself."

Chapter 3

Unused to tropical weather and the added gravity on Patma, the crew tired quickly. The commander ordered them all to rest through the heat of the day. Since most of the crew were spending their nights partying, they were glad for an excuse to nap in the afternoon.

Not Cody. He had to go to bed each night at nine and was up and dressed by seven in the morning. To kill time before breakfast, he would stand at his window and watch a tractor drone clean the beach. The robot scooped up tidal wrack, its arm picked up driftwood, and a rear-mounted rake smoothed away its tread marks.

But no matter how much time he killed, too often Cody was the first person in the dining room. He didn't like eating alone. On the ship, at breakfast, the dining room was always full of people coming off night duty or on their way to work. He missed their company here.

After breakfast he took his camcorder and went biking. He never went far. Riding a bike here took a lot more effort and made him sweat. Sweating was uncomfortable. Sometimes he'd take out an air scooter, but flying alone was still scary.

By nine each morning, he was at his desk studying. By the time he had finished, people were always up. While he ate lunch, they had breakfast and talked about some of the things they'd done the night before—when he'd been sleeping.

Being here, with all new routines, made him feel left out. He'd never felt that way on the ship.

In the afternoon, while the adults slept, he went to the beach. He wasn't supposed to go there alone. It wasn't specifically forbidden—no one knew he went. But Avi had asked him not to leave the hotel grounds alone. Several people had warned him not to talk to strangers if no one from the ship was nearby. Some people, Emory explained, lived in frontier towns because they weren't wanted anywhere else.

I'm not really leaving the grounds, Cody told himself, because the beach is part of the hotel lawn. And it's always deserted, so there aren't any strangers to worry about. Each day he explored a little farther away from the hotel's beach.

He never went swimming—not because he was alone, but because the size of the ocean scared him.

He liked to walk, and watch the waves roll in—as if the water had been programmed never to stop moving. At the water's edge or in the rocky tide pools were endless kinds of new creatures to see. He collected pretty shells and pebbles or just sat and watched animals.

He had no idea what the creatures were called, so he made up names. Small islands offshore were the nesting sites for vast numbers of birds he called orange-chested flyers. They were dark brown with a bright orange breast. From the beach they made the rocky islands appear covered with moving masses of orange flowers.

Perhaps a quarter mile north of the hotel's

true beach, erosion had created a low cliff. In the cliff wall, Cody noticed an odd shadow.

It looked as if there were a hole in the stone at the top of a narrow sloping ledge. Climbing the ledge to see, he discovered the entrance to a tiny cave. He went inside and at once felt more secure.

The cave was cool inside and hardly big enough to hold three people. The floor was covered with silky gray sand. When he sat down and leaned back against the rear wall, he could see a patch of beach and ocean framed by the opening. And no one could see him.

One day, when he got too warm, he went into his cave to cool off. Sitting there in the shade, he watched two large creatures swimming far offshore. After a few minutes he stretched out to rest his eyes from the cloud glare. He didn't know he'd fallen asleep until something woke him.

In a lull between the waves, he heard voices. They sounded very close by, but they weren't human.

He sat up quickly, still not sure the voices weren't part of a dream. A tall wave curled, poured over, and receded with a hiss. A flock of blue scooters darted across the strip of sand framed by the cave mouth. Holding his breath, he waited for the lull between the waves. Just as the quiet ended, he heard a voice, but a wave rolled in and washed the words away.

Patma had no intelligent life-forms. He was sure of that. Otherwise the corporation couldn't have claimed the planet. No one was allowed to claim inhabited worlds. So who was talking? An animal? He knew some birds on Earth could be trained to talk. Or maybe it was some of the strange people he'd been warned about?

Curiosity overcame caution. He crawled closer to the opening. The blue scooters were chasing a frantic school of purple weggie worms left stranded by the last wave. The only other sign of life was his own footprints in the sand.

"Vebbly-blinka-screeb," said something so close by that Cody jumped and hit his head on the cave wall.

"Ow!" The sound escaped before he could think.

"Verda?" something asked softly.

"Kwev?" said another.

Rubbing his sore head, Cody leaned out just far enough to look down over the ledge. Two big creatures standing in the shade of the cliff overhang stared up at him. He stared back, too shocked to make a sound.

Chapter 4

Each creature had five round green eyes. Two big eyes above, mounted on short stalks, and three small eyes below. That was the first thing he noticed. The second was that they had six legs and a long, barrel-shaped body. Their heads were twice the size of his, and oblong. Their *faces,* especially around their eyes, looked like brown velvet. The rest of the head and body was covered with coarse, light brown fur. Stubby antennae, like two big feathers, grew from where ears might have been.

Their legs looked rather like spiders' legs and

were oddly jointed to support the body. The legs were dark brown, smooth as plastic, and ended in a foot with two big front toes and a smaller, thicker toe on the inside. The toes were equipped with long, blunt nails.

He'd seen pictures of Earth animals. These looked nothing like them. He'd been told that all the animals on Patma were hexapeds—they had six legs—and looked strange to human eyes. But nothing had led him to expect animals as strange as this pair. Or as large.

As he stared down at them, each turned one big eye toward the other. Then, to his relief, the creatures began to step backward, slowly and carefully, watching him all the time.

He had never seen any animal here back away; either they ignored people or they came right up to see what you smelled like. These creatures acted as if they were afraid.

"Ssst!" The one on the left raised a front leg and pointed in the direction of the hotel's beach. Its companion nodded as if in agreement. They moved closer together and whispered.

That act alone convinced Cody they were intelligent.

"Don't be scared," he called. "I won't hurt you." At the sound of his voice, one of them began to back away faster.

The cave mouth was small and narrow. By

the time he managed to get to his feet and step out onto the ledge without bumping his head again, the more timid of the pair had almost reached the water.

"Don't be afraid," he called again. "I just want to talk to you." All the time he was thinking that he really shouldn't be doing this. The rules said one never, ever got close to an unknown creature, especially when alone and unarmed.

But these animals *talked,* he thought, which meant they were intelligent. He was pretty sure intelligent creatures—who whispered to each other—wouldn't bite.

The one in the water waited for the next wave to crest before making a graceful floating turn. When it began to swim, it moved its legs like three pairs of oars in a rowboat. Watching it go, Cody realized that it had been these two, or creatures like them, that he'd seen swimming offshore before he fell asleep.

When out a safe distance in the water, the swimmer turned to face the shore and called to its companion. The other one seemed undecided. Twice it raised a foot, then hesitated, glancing from the sea to Cody and back at its companion. It squinched all three of its small eyes together as if worried.

Cody was almost positive they weren't sea

creatures. From everything he'd studied, sea creatures were much more streamlined, and they didn't have legs. They probably weren't insects; he'd never heard of insects talking.

Their eyes were pretty. They reminded him of Avi's jade earrings. The rest of the animal wasn't too attractive, except for those plumelike antennae. But then, he thought, they probably think I look like a monster, too.

He imagined himself as they might see him: short curly dark hair—but only on his head; boots, shorts, and shirt instead of fur. What would they think clothes were? Only two eyes, brown. A nose . . . he couldn't see a nose on the creature. And if it had a mouth, it didn't show on the front of its face. So how did they talk? Or eat? Or hear? Maybe their antennae took the place of ears? And they were taller than he was. . . .

As soon as they were gone, Cody thought, he'd run back to the hotel and tell Avi and the others about his discovery! Maybe no one knew creatures here talked. Almost as soon as that pleasing thought occurred to him, he groaned aloud. He couldn't tell *anyone.* He wasn't supposed to be down here!

The creature below raised its two big eyes in response to his groan.

Admitting he never took an afternoon nap

was nothing compared to admitting that he came out here on the beach alone. Avi almost never got angry at him, but this was sure to be an exception. Especially when she heard about these creatures.

As punishment he might be confined to his room—or worse, sent back to the ship. And it was lonely and boring to be on the ship when all the scientific crew was away.

If Avi were to be reprimanded for something he had done, she might start to resent him . . . as he suspected his parents did. No, he couldn't tell. Even if these talking creatures were an important discovery . . . someone else would get the credit.

The creature below was still watching him. After a bit, it walked a short way up the beach, as if to get a better view of the hotel. When it turned and came walking back toward him, he sensed he was in trouble. It came closer and closer. His heart begin to thud.

Without warning, it reared up on its hindmost legs and, before Cody could move, placed a front leg between him and the cave entrance. Then, with deliberate care, it placed the other front leg so that Cody was penned in. His back was against the cliff, and the animal's face was less than a yard from his.

"Verda," it said softly. Its breath smelled like orange juice. He still couldn't see any mouth. The word seemed to come from its chin, if it had a chin.

In Cody's calm, well-ordered world, no one ever yelled or screamed, and it did not occur to him to do so now. Besides, he was too afraid to make a sound.

"Verda." It touched him gently with the back of its foot, stroking his leg as if to test the strength of his skin.

It was like being petted with a plastic pipe. He jerked away, only to have the other foot close around his waist. He froze, afraid to move for fear of being punctured by the claws.

From offshore, its companion called again, a high-pitched urgent sound. Without warning, Cody felt himself being grasped firmly, lifted up over the antennae, turned in midair, and set down astride the creature's back. He yelled then and struggled, but the creature's grip was firm.

As it wheeled around to face the water, it loosened its right grip, slid the claw down Cody's side, grasped his boot, and forced that foot into the grip of a muscular fold in the side of its short neck. It then let go its grip on his waist.

Cody was trying to pull his foot free when the creature began to run toward the ocean. He had to grab hold of its *fur* to keep from being thrown off and dragged by one leg.

Chapter 5

As the creature waded deeper, warm water poured into Cody's boots and came to his knees. A sudden lunge and his mount began to swim. Powerful muscles moving under Cody swayed him from side to side. He was so busy hanging on that he didn't even notice when his foot came free. By then he was up to his waist in water, afraid of both drowning or falling off and being caught and eaten before he could swim to shore.

Fear jumbled his thoughts. When Avi found

out he was missing, she would be so worried. Emory, too, and others. He had failed Avi by disobeying, by going to the beach alone. What did this creature want from him? If animals here killed and ate people, surely someone would have told him. But what else could it want? If he never came back . . . he couldn't bear to finish that thought.

While these mixed-up thoughts raced on and repeated, he could hear the rhythmic splashing of the creature's swimming, the cries of its companion, and a high-pitched voice calling, "Ah-vee! Ah-vee!" over and over again.

When the creature carrying him caught up with the other, the second creature spashed water in his face. The shock of it made Cody realize that the voice yelling *Ah-vee* was his own. His throat hurt from the effort. He swallowed, glad his mother couldn't see him now—and take pictures. Oddly enough, the thought of her and her camcorder calmed him down. It reminded him of his vow not to show fear.

The two swimmers slowly circled one another, talking in loud voices, as if arguing. Without any warning, the smaller one darted in and struck at Cody. He ducked and yelled. If his mount hadn't dodged, the boy would have been knocked off into the waves.

It was plain to Cody that the smaller, timid one wanted no part of him. It was his kidnapper who wanted to keep him. It did so by turning and swimming rapidly away. The other hurried after them. The shore receded in the distance.

When it seemed to Cody that an hour must have passed and the ride would never end, his mount turned toward shore. Swimming fast, it went rising up and coasting down the waves. Cody hung on, white-knuckled.

They passed between eroded rock formations shaped like four large animals crouching in the water. Currents surged around the rocks. Cody risked a backward glance; the timid one was close behind, body-surfing down a green wave. Seeing its speed and ease in the water, the idea struck Cody that—under different circumstances—this ride might have been fun.

The expert swimmers rode the last wave onto the beach and emerged to run across the sand and scramble up over the dunes.

Behind the dunes, where the soil was thin, stretched miles of scrub growth. There were a few tree-sized plants, but the area was more thicket than forest.

Into this tangle the creatures ran, as if they knew where they were going. Cody had to duck to avoid being hit by branches and fronds.

Looking down, he saw a broad, beaten path below. It was as if they had entered a hallway through the thicket. There was no wind in here. The still air smelled of flowers and a sweet dryness.

The path began to slope downward. Cody braced himself with his knees and leaned back. Not until then did he realize that his right foot was free . . . and had been for quite some time. The animal couldn't swim or run and still keep that muscle fold tight. At the same time as he understood that, he threw himself sideways.

As Cody fell, the creature's front leg accidentally kicked him into the bushes. A middle leg tripped over his boot. Stumbling and trying to stop at the same time caused the creature to fall. The second creature could not stop in time and fell over the first. Where all had been flight and motion a moment before now became a tangle of thrashing legs, breaking branches, and sharp cries.

Ignoring the painful bruises to his hip and leg, Cody rolled over. Before they could stop him, he crawled under the branches on his hands and knees. Pebbles and sticks dug into his skin, but he kept on crawling until branches grew too close to the ground and he could go no farther.

At least they can't get me in here, he thought. They're too big to get in, and their legs aren't long enough to reach in and pull me out. Looking around, he saw a place where he could move deeper into the bushes. If he cleared away dead leaves and branches, he could crawl on his stomach.

And go where? asked his common sense. If he went much farther, he might get lost. From here he could get back to the path, follow the path to the beach, and follow the beach back to the hotel. Once the animals went away, of course.

That decided, he felt much better. All he had to do was wait—and move the rock pressing into his right knee. Such close quarters made any movement difficult. Shifting his weight from his knees to his hands, he stretched out on his stomach, then rolled onto his side. Now he had a clear view back to the path and could see up through the branches.

The path seemed empty at the moment, but on the twigs and leaves overhead were hundreds of little moving things, like half-beads fringed with tiny legs. Black beads, brown, yellow, tan—all shiny, all hurrying about in their hidden world. He saw that the leaves were lacy with holes. Perhaps these things ate leaves? All he knew about insects came from biology lessons.

A black bead landed on his arm and stumbled along over the hairs. It made him itch and he flicked it off. Another one landed on his neck and walked. He brushed at it, then felt a wet, crinkly spot and knew, to his disgust, that he'd crushed it. The wet spot burned. Rubbing the spot made his fingertip burn. He rubbed his finger on his shorts, then into the sand. The sand eased the burn. He rubbed sand on his neck.

Six big legs walked slowly down the path. He could see only as high as their knees. They were odd knees, like ball joints. The smaller animal walked by, going the other way. The pair was looking for him. They began talking softly and, although he wanted to listen, his attention was distracted.

The little beadlike things were coming down out of the branches overhead. Flying or floating, it was hard to say which, but they were landing on him. He could feel them in his hair. Wherever they touched bare skin, they caused an itch that quickly became a burn. He wanted to smash them, but remembering how the first one burned made him control the urge.

He shook his leg. A few bugs fell to the ground, but most landed on his other leg. More drifted down. He could endure the burning sensation on his arms and legs but having them on his face finally broke his self-control.

"Arrugh!"

At his cry of distress and disgust, a velvety head appeared at an opening under the bushes. The pupils of its five eyes widened in the dimness. Locating him, it seemed to study him for a moment, then carefully shielded its eyes with one foot.

The head turned at an angle, and Cody saw a glimpse of open mouth. And teeth—wide, flat, pale brown teeth, outlined by shiny brown lips that looked like they were trying to whistle when the creature spoke. He shivered at the strangeness.

"Ver standig!" it said, softly coaxing. "Ver. Ver." It backed away and gestured with its foot for him to come out.

If he was going to die, he thought—without truly believing death was possible—he preferred it to be quick rather than being acid-burned to death by these little things. He backed out the way he'd come, trying not to mash bugs as he moved. Even so, by the time he reached the path and stood up, his arms and legs were burning so painfully that involuntary tears filled his eyes.

The creatures were waiting for him. One immediately gripped his arms and turned him to face the other. "Cut it out!" he cried. They ignored him, which was a good thing. For then they proceeded to de-bead him.

One ruffled his hair to shake the insects loose. The other used a claw like a dull knife, carefully drawing it down his arms and legs, lifting the insects off and flicking them away. All the time they worked, they made sounds to each other or to him. He couldn't be sure, but they seemed to be trying to comfort him. Would they bother to do this if they were going to hurt him?

When they were done, they let go of him. He stood between them on the path and checked his arms and legs. His skin was dotted and streaked with tiny white blisters like acid burns. The animals were talking to each other, as if debating what to do. His burns hurt so much that he was too miserable to care what they did with him.

The larger animal turned and started down the path, going deeper into the brush. Cody was watching it go when he felt a gentle push and then another.

"Stop it!"

The animal said something.

"You know I can't understand you! Let me go! I have to go to the beach and wash off this burning acid!"

When he tried to slip past, the creature simply raised its front legs, like a person extending his arms. He dodged right, then left, then right again. Each time it stopped him. There was no way past, except by crawling back under the bushes. With a groan of despair that was half a sob, he gave up and went where they wanted him to go.

CHAPTER 6

To Cody it was the place of caves. Wide openings, like half circles, led into the side of a thicketed hill. In front of the doors, a pathway meandered along under the canopy of branches. There was a strange smell in the air, not unpleasant, but distinct. He couldn't tell if it came from the caves or the flowers.

Flowering plants like big blue orchids bloomed between the doorways. Seeing the flowers made Cody wonder if the creatures had planted them as decoration. To the left of the path, narrow trails led down to a swiftly flowing river just visible through the leaves.

If people search for me, they'll never find me here, he thought, and his heart sank. From the air, these pathways wouldn't be visible or they would look like natural clearings.

Sweat was making his blisters burn more. He wiped his face on his sleeves and wondered if people could die from heat and pain.

As they passed the caves, more creatures like the pair escorting Cody emerged from the doorways. He could hear them mumbling among themselves. There were so many! All sizes and colors. It was like a town. Now and then his escorts spoke but kept on walking. He was herded down a path to the river.

When they pointed to a sandbar where he could sit and wash his burning skin, Cody needed no translation. The water felt so cool and good. Scrubbing with wet sand was painful but removed the burning sensation. Stopping the pain was such a relief that minutes passed before he looked up. The riverbank was rimmed with creatures—all watching him.

When he stared back, some moved away nervously. Three of the creatures stood close by, as if guarding him. None of them looked like the two who had captured him, but he couldn't be sure. To his alien eyes they all looked very much alike.

His stomach cramped at the sound of what could only be termed shouting from the hillside above. Either there was going to be a fight . . . or they were preparing something terrible for him. Or maybe both? The water wasn't deep. Maybe he should try to run away down the river? He stood up, water pouring from the pockets of his shorts. A creature walked into the stream to block his way.

The creatures didn't know whether to watch him or what was going on behind them. Some tried doing both, turning their heads as if at a tennis match or raising their uppermost eyes to their fullest extension.

From the hillside above, someone said, "Subba dee," or what sounded like that. It was repeated three times, each time louder. A voice he recognized as belonging to one of his captors answered. It sounded like a long explanation. The other captor's voice joined in.

"E subba dee?" the loud voice said again.

"Sa."

"Fribbinsh!"

The loud one was talking to his captors! And unless Cody was mistaken, they were being reprimanded. Which might mean they shouldn't have brought him here. He hoped that was what was happening.

The loud voice called out something. One of his guards answered. When Cody looked at the guard, it lifted a foot and pointed up the hill. When Cody didn't move, the creature motioned with the foot and spoke, clearly wanting him to go up there.

Cody looked around. He was almost surrounded. There was no way to make a break for it and run. He took a deep breath. "Might as well get it over with," he said, and started toward the riverbank. Water in his boots squished with each step. Either out of courtesy or fear, the creatures stepped back, giving him lots of room to pass, then followed him up the hill.

In the clearing in front of a wide cave door, his two captors faced a very large, dark yellow member of their kind. The eyes of the honey-colored creature raised to watch Cody approach—as if, Cody thought, its eyes were twin camera lenses. He lifted his chin and walked up and stood beside his two captors.

"Hello." He didn't expect an answer.

"You will be taken back to your kind," Honey-color said quite clearly. The voice was low, the inflection so strange that the words seemed to have a different meaning. There were *s*'s in words that had no *s* in them.

As soon as he understood what he'd just heard, Cody gave a little "Yes!" of joy and relief. "Do you mean it? I can go back?"

"Yess," came the hissed response. "You must go back."

Cody felt as if he could run and jump and scream for joy—but not think too clearly. "How do you know our language? No one said there were animals here that could talk."

Distress was making him tactless, and he blushed. "I'm sorry. I know you must have some word for yourselves. Like we're called humans. I . . . uh, how did you learn to speak our language? Is this where you live?"

The creature let him blither on until he fell silent with self-consciousness. Even then it said nothing, but simply watched him. The two beside Cody stood completely still, all eyes fixed on what was plainly their superior.

"You will be taken back," the big creature repeated slowly, adding, "Your being here puts us in danger. I am sad that these two caused you fear and pain. Humans never come into the thickets because of the bleemies." One foot pointed at his blisters. "Please do not cause your people to get even with us for bringing you here."

"I wouldn't do that," Cody said, not sure what the creature meant by *get even.* "But can I go soon, please? Before Avi—anyone finds out I'm gone?"

"Yess, that would be good." The creature spoke as if it had to think a while to remember the right words.

Able to think more clearly now that he was less frightened, Cody repeated his question. "Why can you speak our language and these two can't?"

"They do not know your language. Only . . . I do . . . remember. They brought you here because they had never seen young of your kind. The lack of . . . *human* young was a puzzle to us. Are there other young here?"

"No . . . only me." Cody didn't know why saying that made him sad. "There are children on Earth, our home world."

"Do you also claim that you come from the stars?"

"Yes . . . in a way." Cody didn't know how to make this creature understand. "I was born in a cruiser—a ship that travels deep space." To explain about the lack of other children, he wanted to add that he wasn't supposed to have been born. That seemed demeaning to himself, so he changed the subject. "You didn't say yet how you learned our language. And why didn't anyone tell me about you—that all of you live here?"

Before the creature could answer Cody, someone in the crowd spoke. The leader responded in their language. Another voice was heard, and the leader spoke again, as if answering questions. Finally its attention returned to Cody.

"Fast then," it said. "You cannot stay here. I do not know why you were not told of us. When your kind and your machines first came, I was small. Trusting. Curious. The small learn quickly if they watch and listen."

Cody was thinking that the first expedition had landed on Patma almost three hundred Earth years before. "Excuse me, but how old are you?"

"That old," the creature said and went on. "Humans made a pet of me. They called me Skipper. They put a green box on my tle—my leg." It raised its right foreleg slightly. "I thought it was a gift, but they put such gifts on others and made the boxes come alive. Made us sick and dizzy. We pulled the boxes off and ran away. They stunned us and brought us back."

"They put transmitters on you," Cody said, explaining things as much to himself as to the creature. "To track you. To see where you lived, what you ate . . . But transmitters shouldn't make an ani——make you dizzy unless the frequency . . . Like sharks can't wear them . . ." He sputtered to a halt, not knowing how to explain. "Why didn't our people just talk to you?"

Jewellike amber eyes studied him. "Your kind does not listen to others. Pets. To them, only humans can think or feel."

Some of the crew called him a pet, Cody thought. And many never really listened to him, either. As if, because of his age, they thought he was stupid. They were always kind to him, though. The creature gestured as if waiting for him to say something.

"Couldn't you tell them what you were? Didn't they hear you all talking?" The unfairness of what he was hearing made Cody forget his own situation.

"We did tell them. They did not want to know. Parroting, they said our talk was. I do not know the meaning." The big creature hissed, a scary sound to Cody, although it could have been the equivalent of a human sigh or a sort of wry laughter. He wasn't sure he believed this story. The people he knew wouldn't act this way.

"In the beginning I knew only some of your words," the big creature said. "Two others of our kind spoke more. The humans killed them."

"They killed some of you *because* you talked?" Cody wanted to make sure he understood. "As punishment?"

"To study us, they said. To take apart into small pieces to study."

With a sickening little thrill of horror, Cody understood. The first expedition to land on Patma had killed—it was called collecting—some of these creatures as specimens. It was common practice for expeditions to collect samples of alien life-forms. In the labs on the *Annie Cannon* he had seen hundreds of such specimens, frozen whole or as tissue samples on slides. But no sentient creatures, meaning those with intelligence, were ever supposed to be killed. That was against the law. Or so he had been told. What had happened here? And why?

"I was put into a pen and kept where all could see," the big creature continued. "I feared being killed also. There in that pen I learned many words but was afraid to speak them. Because of the killings, none of us spoke again where humans could hear."

"I'm sorry all that happened," Cody said. His apology sounded lame even to him. "People must have been different then. I don't know anyone who would act that way. The people on my ship are good. They get very excited about any new life-forms they find. They—" His speech, if understood, was ignored.

"Before the humans went away, I was set free," the creature continued. "They entered their gray-and-blue box. It went up into the sky and did not return. Three more of my friends went with them. Dead. In sacks. Time passed. We forgot our fear. Then other humans came. They had removable skins of a different color. They caused more death, of our kind and others. I hid and listened. Learned more of your words. These humans called us all skippers. I do not know why."

The skipper paused in its story and seemed to tense. Its big eyes searched the sky, and its antennae stood almost straight up. Then it spoke to the group in its own tongue, a quick, harsh comment. Whatever it said made the others run inside their doors as fast as they could.

Cody was looking up at the sky, trying to figure out what was wrong, when he suddenly found himself being picked up again—by the honey-colored skipper. Just as he was being carried into a cave, he saw a flash of bright red. It was a red security car flying in the distance.

"They're looking for me!" he said. "They're searching along the beach! I'll run down there! They can pick me up!"

The skipper put him down but hooked a claw through the waistband of Cody's shorts. "And follow you back here, where they will kill us all. No. You will stay here."

Chapter 7

"You promised!" Cody fought back tears of disappointment and fear. "That's not fair! You said I could go. They won't come back here. I won't tell on you. I'll say I got lost exploring the beach."

The skipper did not relax its grip. "From the human town to this place is far. They will not believe you walked so far. Climbed the gelbare . . . the cliffs."

"You can't keep me here," Cody said, feeling desperate. He suspected they could keep him if they wanted to.

"Until dark," said the skipper. "When dark comes I will take you back." He gave Cody a little shake to keep him from interrupting again. "No more talk. I must think."

It spoke to a rust-colored skipper who had followed them in. That skipper promptly positioned itself in the doorway. Cody's host unhooked its claw, saying, "If you try to escape, Ssart will stop you."

The guard didn't look at all friendly. Its large right eye and stalk were missing, the face disfigured by an ugly scar.

"Would Ssart kill me?" Cody asked. When the honey-colored skipper did not answer, he whirled around to find it was no longer in the cave. It hadn't gone out the door, so where was it?

The high-domed room was dimly lit, but Cody thought he could see another opening, way at the back of the cave. It must have gone out that way. He started to go look, then glanced back at Ssart and changed his mind.

Suddenly aware of being very tired, he sat down on the floor. There was nothing else to sit on. The sand felt cool against his burned legs. After pushing sand into a pillow mound, he stretched out, cradling his head in his hands.

Could he trust the skipper to take him back when night came? Did he have any choice? They had no lighting here—none that he'd seen anyway. He'd never been where there were no lights. No technology. The thought of being here in the dark was scary.

He couldn't blame the skippers for being afraid of humans, he decided. If an alien came and collected people as specimens, he'd be scared, too, and hate them. Why had that first crew done that when they knew skippers talked? And why wasn't there any mention of skippers in the data that the *Annie Cannon*'s crew was given before coming here? Maybe the skippers hid so well that people thought they were extinct. That might explain it.

A rustling noise made Cody glance toward the door. Ssart was sitting on its rump, middle legs folded over its stomach. With its front feet it was twisting vines together, using the short, inside toe like a thumb. The trailing ends writhed in the dust as it worked. Almost as if it were making a rope . . . did skippers use ropes? To tie people up? Ssart stopped what it was doing and stared back at him.

Cody sat up, feeling less vulnerable that way.

The guard shifted uneasily and turned its head to peer at him with one stalked eye. Did the top eyes see better?

"I was just looking," Cody said, and looked

up at the ceiling instead. His vision had adjusted to the dim light. To his surprise, he saw that the ceiling wasn't just rock but carved and decorated rock.

Like a bicycle wheel, perfectly even lines radiated from a perfect circle. Inside the spokes were carved pictures of animals—many-legged, bug-eyed creatures, like none he'd ever seen. Yet. They crowded the space, all seeming to rush away from the hub. Where the domed ceiling met the wall, the wheel was rimmed with pictures of skippers, like a border frieze around the room.

Could skippers have carved this? He looked back at Ssart, who was now braiding the vines . . . using thumbs . . .

"They use tools!" he whispered to himself. The implications of that thought shocked him so much he jumped up. "They talk and use tools. So why are there people on this planet?"

Language and tool-making and use were signs of a sentient species, creatures with intelligence. If people found creatures like that on a planet, that meant the planet was off-limits. Humans might visit and study, but could not stay. Building a town and hotels, mining—all that would be against the law. Or so he had been taught.

Excited by his thoughts, he got up and

walked along the curving wall, studying the carvings, wondering. He came to the opening in the rear wall, and it was almost a surprise; he'd forgotten about that exit. Cool air currents breathed from the roughly arched opening. It was too dark to see what the passage was like, but in the distance was a patch of yellow-green light. Sunlight on leaves at the end of a tunnel? The big skipper had gone out that way. So the passage might lead outside.

Maybe the skippers won't take me back tonight, he thought. If they're this smart, maybe the big one will decide it's too dangerous and keep me here. No one at the hotel knows where I am. The skippers could just kill me and hide my body.

The way his stomach cramped at that idea made Cody decide to make a run for it. To try to escape down that tunnel. If it led outside, and the skippers were still in their caves hiding from the security car, he might get away.

Cody walked past the archway as casually as he could, glancing back at Ssart. It was still busy twisting vines and seemed to be paying no attention to him. Now was a good time to run . . . except if the passage did lead outside, there might be a guard at the other end, too. His stomach cramped again.

Maybe there wasn't another guard? It was

worth the chance. He whirled around, darted through the archway, and ran.

The floor sloped down. The sand was slippery under his boot soles. In spite of the dim glow ahead, he could hardly see. The air grew thick and smelled like rotting plants. The farther he went, the more he suspected that coming in here was a serious mistake.

He gave a little moan of pain when he ran hard against a wall and bounced off, scuffing his arm and nearly falling. Stumbling aside, he saw the passage curved. There was more green light ahead, enough to see it wasn't sunlight on leaves.

Sure now that he shouldn't have come down here, he slowed to look back. There were four pale green lights, one large and three small, coming after him. It was too late to change his mind.

Cody entered the huge green cavern at a dead run. As he passed between two massive pillars, a clawed arm reached out, closed around his waist, and jerked him up so that he ran on air. His screams echoed and re-echoed.

"Stop it! Stop it!" The skipper shook him impatiently before lowering him to the ground. "How dare you enter here! Stop your barbaric noise! This is our szirpac."

The word had no meaning to Cody. Having

quit yelling when his feet touched the floor, he twisted sideways, frantic to break free. The skipper abruptly let go, and the boy fell onto the sandy floor. For a time he knelt, doubled over, panting with exertion and fear, rubbing his bruised ribs. Then he forced himself to look up, an act of sheer will because he was so frightened.

"It's you!"

To his surprise, his captor was not Ssart but the leader. Its eyes glowed oddly in this light; its antennae and fur were tinged with green, its legs shiny with green highlights. From where Cody knelt it looked huge and powerful and very alien.

In its own language it spoke to Ssart. Until then Cody hadn't been aware the other skipper was standing right behind him. He flinched, needlessly. In answer to the superior, the guard turned and left.

For what seemed like a long time, the big skipper stared down at him, as if unsure what to do. Cody waited in dread. He could hear water dripping somewhere in the cavern.

Finally the skipper spoke. "Here we keep the images of what was and what will be forever— or what we once believed would be forever— until your kind came to spoil our world. You will show respect here. Even if you feel only contempt."

"I'm sorry," Cody whispered. "You scared me. That's why I screamed. I didn't mean to insult you. I only wanted to get out. To go back." He didn't know what else to say. "Can I stand up, please?"

"Yess, yess." The skipper's tone was softer, as if it might have been sorry, too. It waited while Cody pushed himself to his feet and brushed the sand off his knees.

"Tell me, young human," the skipper said then, "how would you feel if we invaded your world and treated you as your kind treat us?"

Embarrassed by the fact that his knees were shaking, Cody was in no frame of mind for a philosophical chat. Still, he was too scared not to answer. "I've thought about that," he said. "I've never seen my world, but if you came aboard our ship and did that, I'd be very scared. And very angry."

"How could you not see your own world?" asked the skipper, distracted from its original question.

"Because I was born in the ship—in space."

"Why are there no other young 'born in space'?"

"It's forbidden . . . especially on research ships."

"It's forbidden—but you were allowed to live." It wasn't a question, and Cody didn't know what to say. "You are special," the skipper added softly.

"No . . . well, yes, but just in that way."

The skipper didn't respond. As the silence continued, Cody became more aware of the sweetish scent of the cavern. The longer he was in there, the more noticeable it became. Not quite sickening, but almost. He wanted to get out.

If the outer chamber was intricately decorated, this room was phantasmagoric. Everything was round. Pillars like stacks of carved balls supported the carved ceiling. Some of the balls were carved so that there were balls within balls, each depicting one animal or tree or flower or thing, repeated over and over. Walls, ceiling, alcoves—all were carved in bewildering intricacy.

Thrusting up from trenches lining every wall were masses of bulbous growths glowing with greenish light. Woven baskets, hung from the ceiling like living chandeliers, overflowed with masses of the glowing stuff.

"What is that?" Cody pointed to a basket.

"Your word is *fungus.*"

"Why do they give off light?"

"They live where it is dark."

"Oh." Then he remembered the proper words

for living things that emitted light: *bioluminescent* and *phosphorescent.*

"And these carvings, what do they mean?"

"You will not understand."

"Not if you don't tell me. Who carved this?"

"Our . . . *people,* long ago."

"How . . . with what tools?"

"Sand. Vines. Stone that your kind calls diamond. And these." It clenched its front claws. "Over lifetimes."

"How do you carve with vines?" Cody asked. The hobby shop on the ship stocked all sorts of lasers for carving.

"When a certain vine is stripped of its . . . skin, it bleeds with . . . sticky juice. Crushed sand or diamonds are put on the wet vines, and they are allowed to dry. They work like this." With its front feet the skipper mimed sawing with a vine.

Cody thought that over. It was clever, but primitive. "It would take so long to carve that way," he said.

"There was no need to hurry."

"But what do you do in here?" Cody asked.

The skipper hissed in what could have been irritation. "The szirpacs are the place where we show honor to the creator of our world and all that is."

"This is your chapel . . ." Cody guessed,

"your church . . . a sacred place? Where you come to pray?"

"You know about such places?" The skipper seemed surprised and very interested. "Your kind has them?"

"Yes. There's an all-faiths chapel in the ship. People go there to pray . . . and to think, too."

"You honor the creator of your ship?"

Only good manners kept the boy from giggling. "Some people might, I don't know. Earth has lots of religions. But most have a creator in them," he added, glad to find a common bond.

"Those of your kind who have come here, do they honor the creator?"

"Some do I guess." Cody didn't remember seeing any chapels in the town, but then he hadn't looked for any.

"If they honor the creator of their world," said the skipper, "why do they dishonor ours?"

"Do you mean by treating you badly?"

"By treating all of our world badly," said the skipper. "To hurt or destroy one is to hurt all. Each one is special. Each one matters. So we believe. That is what this place shows."

It walked over and, with a claw-tip, lightly tapped an image on the nearest pillar. "This creature could not live without that one." The claw tapped. "And the next above would die without this one." The claw tapped a third image. "All three could not live without this one and this one. If one died out, all would die. Just as surely as if this ball was broken, the pillar would fall. If many pillars fell, the roof would fall. This place would be gone forever.

"So it is with our world. Your kind is destroying what the creator gave us. Because all is one, pieces of our life are being taken away forever. When you take stones and trees and seashells, you destroy us bit by bit. Each thing destroyed or taken to your world diminishes ours. If this goes on, there will come a time when the damage is irreparable. Our world will die. We will die."

The skipper fell silent. Cody didn't know what to say and so kept quiet.

"In the . . . songs from the past," the skipper said then, "the stories passed on by the old to the young since time began, there is nothing to predict this. The songs promise forever."

Chapter 8

They walked back up to the entrance room together, Cody and the skipper. "I will take you back," the creature assured him several times, "but you must wait until it is safe for us. They fly over. Listen."

Cody could hear the whine of an accelerating air car from somewhere nearby. That there were people out there made him feel better. He took a deep breath; the air smelled much fresher here. "What do I do until then?" he asked.

The skipper had to think about that. "Rest. Sleep. Here." It pointed to the floor. "You are safe. We have made you . . . your day bad. I am sorry you were carried here by that young . . . *skipper.*" The last word sounded like an insult.

Cody smiled nervously. It didn't occur to him until later that the skippers would have no idea what a smile meant.

Had he been offered a wager he would have bet anything that he wouldn't sleep here. But he did. Even with Ssart at the entrance again, he fell into a deep sleep almost as soon as he lay down.

Waking up was bad. It was almost dark. At first he didn't know where he was. He gave a yelp of fear and rolled away at being touched by claws. Something big loomed over him.

"Quiet! Quiet!" Hearing the voice, he remembered. "You are safe," the skipper said.

Outside the air smelled fresh and was so cool he was almost cold. The only lights were stars visible between the leaves. He couldn't see or hear any other skippers.

"Where is everyone? Have they gone to bed?" he asked, then thought, what else was there to do here?

"Follow me."

The big creature was a moving blackness on the pale sand of the path. Cody had to jog to keep up, but he didn't mind. He was going back! Remembering the insects, he was careful to stay away from the bushes. Twice he thought he heard noises behind them, but when he looked back could see nothing in the dark. He decided it was probably the wind blowing over the thicket. By the time he could hear the surf, he was sweating from the run.

"Just tell me which way to go," he said as they climbed over the dune. "I can find my way back."

What he desperately wanted at the moment was privacy. For the past few hours he had needed to go to the bathroom. The sound of the waves was pure torture.

"There are cliffs—"

"I'll be fine. Really."

"No. You are special to your kind. We are responsible. I will carry you there. . . . Listen!" About to lift him up, the skipper paused. Antennae waving briskly, it walked a few steps back toward the dune and peered upward. Cody looked, too.

"Rehorbs botha!"

Cody jumped, startled by the cry. As the other skippers crested the dune, all he could see at first was a forest of antennae, like black feathers moving against the night sky. As they ran down over the sand toward him, he saw there were at least a dozen.

"Rehorbs!" other voices cried. They were loud, perhaps from excitement or from an effort to be heard above the crash of the waves.

"What is it?" he called. "What are they saying? What do they want?"

"They are saying, 'Come back.' They want to keep you," the big skipper called to him over the noise. There was jostling in the crowd and sharp cries of what sounded like pain as the leader pushed and elbowed its way back to where Cody stood.

"Why?" Fear erased all other thought.

"To make all humans agree to leave our world forever. You are special—" The skipper broke off to push away several others crowding too near. "The only child. They think your people would agree to anything to get you back."

"They're wrong!" Cody was hoping they were right. "Besides, if you kept me here, what could I eat? Or drink? I can't even drink your water. Tell them that!"

"They know that. They think, to save your life, humans would soon agree to leave our world."

"No!" How could he convince them they were wrong when they had seen the air cars searching for him all afternoon? "You don't know people. They wouldn't go. Once they knew you had me, they'd come and get me—anyway they could."

"Would they kill us?" his skipper asked.

". . . they might." Cody wasn't sure if that were true, but hearing it made the leader give a long speech to the others.

Not knowing their language, Cody couldn't tell what made some of the group try to interrupt his skipper's speech. One of the creatures standing near Cody muttered something angrily. When Cody looked at it, the creature lunged and took a swipe at him.

"Ouch!" Cody ducked as claws whipped across his hair, catching strands and yanking them out. At his cry, the honey-colored skipper and then two others quickly positioned themselves between Cody and his attacker.

Other voices cried out or hissed. Somebody struck one of his protectors. He could hear the thud of the blow. A fight broke out. Legs hit legs, claws clacked together on impact. It was too dark to see what was happening. To avoid being hit or stepped on as his protectors moved, he had to keep dodging.

When a strip of open sand appeared and Cody saw the white line of foam beyond, he made a break for it. Too desperate to worry that he could be grabbed by a dozen different skippers, he sprinted through the opening and kept running.

He dodged behind the first big rock he came to, to get out of their sight. Considering their eyes and the dimness of their caves, he was pretty sure they could see better than he could in the dark. More rocks lay ahead; he zigzagged among them.

His boots were still wet. Designed for a spaceship and never intended for running or rugged outdoor wear, getting dunked in the ocean had made them shrink. Cody didn't even feel the fabric rubbing against the blisters on his feet.

The first cliff was a low outcropping, like a breakwater. Scrambling to the top he looked back and saw maybe eight or ten skippers following. One was much too close. In the dark they looked like great black spiders hurrying across the sand. One heart-stopping glimpse was enough. Not pausing to catch his breath, he set off again.

The next cliff was much higher. Climbing up its ledges reminded him of Patma's gravity and of how tired and thirsty he was. By the time he reached the top, he had a painful stitch in his side but didn't dare stop. That lead skipper was gaining.

He ran on, stumbling often, bent over clutching his side. He was desperately hoping to find a place to hide—to catch his breath and stop the pain.

The rocks up here were so dark he couldn't see his feet. Maybe if he just dropped flat on the ground the night would hide him? In the dark his shorts and shirt looked black. But that would work only if the skippers lacked night vision. A quick glance back and down, and he dismissed that idea. The skippers were running, and starting to climb, as if they were having no trouble seeing.

Cody gave a small moan of despair, thinking how far he was from the hotel and how alone. He might as well give up. "Giving up gets you nothing," Avi always said whenever he complained about something being too difficult. Remembering that convinced him to keep on running.

Wildlife slept or nested on these cliffs. He could hear animals run away squeaking as he passed by. Coarse sea grass grew here, covering the sand and rocks with wiry runners. Twice he tripped and nearly fell. The third runner he kicked into was so firmly anchored that it threw him sprawling. He fell so hard, the wind was knocked out of him, and all he could do was lie there, stunned.

Seabirds nesting on the ledges flew up in a panic of wingbeats and circled overhead, uttering piercing cries, scaring him more. If the skippers hadn't seen where he fell, the birds were telling them. For a moment he hated those birds.

Sea wind ruffled his hair, and he shivered. Then in the lull between waves, he heard skippers talking at the base of the ledge. Their feet made whispering scratches as they climbed. The sound made the hair on his arms stand up, and he shivered again, this time not from cold.

His hands had taken the worst of his fall. When he tried to get up, he had to scrape pebbles and grit out of his palms before pushing himself to his knees. His left knee hurt and when he touched it, it felt sticky with blood and sand.

Pebbles crunched on the rocks behind him. Cody turned to see a skipper—so close there was no chance to run, just to duck down as it moved over him.

"Quiet!" Using a middle foot, the skipper firmly pressed him flat into the grass again, until Cody could smell the stone beneath his face. "Stay still," it added unnecessarily. Cody had no intention of moving. The sweet-acid breath of the whisper jetted over his ear and cheek.

"They do not see you. I will lead them away," the skipper said. "When you can, run toward the red moon rising now over your . . . town." A foot lightly patted his back, as if to reassure. "I am ss-sorry," the skipper added. "I do not want them to keep you."

"Ssorpress!" The cry was so loud and unexpected that Cody's heart skipped a beat. *"Ssorpress!"* the skipper called again. Pebbles flew as it suddenly spurted away from him and ran off into the night. At least three other skippers ran past, so close he could hear their feet ripping the vines.

"Ssorpress!" The word was shouted by other voices before the next wave slapped against and poured over the rocks below. By the time Cody could hear them again, the voices seemed far down the beach.

In the miasma of his fear, minutes passed before he truly understood that the skipper had deliberately fooled the others and led them away. Relief and gratitude flooded over him, and his eyes filled with tears.

And then he reminded himself that he wouldn't be out here like this, alone in the night of an alien world, if it weren't for skippers. Still, the big skipper seemed kind. If they'd met some other way, they might have become friends. Maybe.

When it seemed safe, he got up and looked around. Moving took effort; he hurt all over. There was the red moon—a dim, rusty sphere just above the horizon. The shifting line of white foam that marked the beach below seemed to lead right to the moon. Light glowed in the sky between here and the horizon . . . the town! He began to walk, all else forgotten but his need to get back to where there were people.

Soon after climbing down to the beach, his hopes soared at seeing the green running lights of an air car as it rose into view in the distance.

They were still hunting for him, even though it was dark! To his intense disappointment the air car returned to land almost at once. A taxi from the port? Other lights appeared and disappeared as quickly. People going home from the town, he guessed. After several more such disappointments, he quit watching the sky and trudged along, cold and hungry.

He walked wherever walking was easiest, usually along the edge of the wave line, where the wet sand was hard-packed.

Large flocks of seabirds rested there. At his approach they moved away like gray shadows on the sand. If he came too close, they flew. After passing several flocks, he realized that he could smell them before he could see them—a salty, slightly rancid odor. Most were visible only because they moved.

Twice he disturbed large scavengers that growled, then sniffed and fled into the night, as leery of his strangeness as he was of theirs. He circled away from what they had been feeding on; the dead things smelled sickening. There were noises from the ocean, too; not only the slurp and gurgle of waves around rocks but snorts and whistles and breathings, as if aquatic animals followed him, hidden by the dark water.

Until tonight he hadn't realized there were this many animals on Patma. He seldom saw any during the day, around the hotel. On the hotel beach, most animals came out only when there were no people around.

Either he was too tired to notice or a rock outcropping ahead hid the approach of the air car. A blindingly bright searchlight suddenly swept the beach and passed over him.

"Hey!" he said, startled. "I'm here!" He whirled around and saw the car gliding out over the water. The heaving waves were deep green beneath the misty cone of light. Seabirds riding the waves flew up in panic; diamonds of water flashed from their wings.

The car was making too wide a circle. They hadn't seen him! "Hey! Come back! I'm here!" he shouted again and again. "Come back! You missed me!"

The car was heading back to the north. First the cone of light disappeared behind the rocks ahead, and then he couldn't see the car. They were going back to town! They didn't see him. "You missed me! Come back!"

His shrill cry of disappointment was suddenly joined by the whine of the air car's acceleration. The searchlight swept back over the rocks, turning the sand white, casting his long, frantically waving shadow behind him as the car again sped out over the water.

Cody spun around and watched the air car make a tight circle to the south. When it turned so the light was aimed back at him, he shouted, "Yes!" and cheered the car's return by waving wildly with both hands and jumping up and down.

"Here I am! Down here!" The light moved away from him to sweep back and forth over the beach. He kept on waving and yelling long after he was sure they were going to land.

With yellow lights blinking and landing signal beeping, the car put down only yards away. Pearly white letters emblazoned on its side said SECURITY. Beneath that was stenciled a black *#9—Patma Center.*

The car's dome light gleamed off Avi's hair as the hatch slid back and she jumped down to the sand. For him that moment was the equivalent of "coming home." He ran over and threw his arms around her neck. She smelled so good, so familiar!

Avi hugged him so tightly, his bruised sides hurt and he could hardly breathe, but he didn't care. She was crying—something he'd never seen her do. Her tears more than anything else told him how upset she had been.

"Are you all right?" she kept repeating, although Cody assured her he was. "I was so worried," she said. "We all were. Everyone's been out hunting for you. We couldn't imagine what had happened. Did someone—"

"I got lost," Cody said quickly. "I couldn't sleep and I was bored, so I went for a walk—and got lost." As he told the lie, it seemed to him a week had passed since that afternoon. "I followed a path into the bushes. And I got acid-burned by bugs in there . . . and then, when I found the beach again, I just started following it back. Are you okay, Avi? Please don't cry. I'm sorry to worry you so much."

"How did you know which way to walk on the beach?" Avi searched her pockets for a tissue and blew her nose.

"The town lights up the sky above it."

"But that's after dark! You've been gone ten hours."

"Have I?" Cody was too tired to think of a logical explanation for the time delay. "I just took a chance. I figured if I stuck to the beach someone would find me."

The white-uniformed officer piloting the air car didn't bother to get out, nor did she return Cody's "Hi" as the boy climbed into the rear seat with Avi. "He's on board now. No. No.

Seems unhurt. I'm coming in," the pilot informed the radio.

The hatch slid shut, closing out the sound of the waves, and for a second all was silent. Cody noticed there was an interesting array of equipment in the car, including what appeared to be a folded net and restraining devices that pulled out from the sides of the seat. The car smelled of dust, simu-leather, and old sweat.

Instead of taking off, the pilot half turned and stared back over the seat at Cody. The leathery skin of the woman's round face was shiny and sun-splotched by years of neglect. "You O.K., kid?" she said finally, her tone mildly sarcastic.

"Fine, thank you."

"You're sure about that?"

"Yes."

"Good." There was an awkward pause. "You ever consider wearing a chroncom?"

"I wasn't planning to get lost."

Sensing Cody's growing discomfort, Avi suggested, "Perhaps we should get back to the center?"

"Yeah. He's the first kid I've seen in twenty-three years. I forgot how short they were." With a sniff of dismissal she turned back to the controls. "But then, he's big enough to give us a long hard day."

"I'm sorry," Cody apologized again. "It wasn't on purpose."

"Never is with kids," the pilot said. "That's why I left mine back on Earth with their grandparents."

Chapter 10

Raucous cheers, whistles, and applause greeted them as Cody and Avi walked into the crowded hotel lounge. All this attention made Cody feel good, if rather embarrassed. He'd never seen some of these people before.

"Thank you," he said, feeling awkward in front of the strangers. "I'm glad to be back . . . that's very nice of you."

"You bet it is, Little Bit." Emory stepped forward to give him a quick hug. "Welcome home," he said.

Cody grinned up at him, so glad to see him that he didn't even mind being called Little Bit.

People crowded around, asking how he was, sympathizing with his bruises and bleemie burns, questioning Avi. To his relief no one seemed angry that he had caused so much trouble. They just sounded glad that he was back safely.

In her role as physician, Avi soon cut short the welcoming fuss. "This can all wait until morning," she said. "Cody needs some first aid, some dinner, and rest."

"Excuse me." Unable to wait until they left before he went to the bathroom, Cody began to work his way through the crowd. "Excuse me." People started to laugh when they guessed where he was headed. That was embarrassing, too, but he was too desperate to care at the moment.

"Why didn't you go on the beach?" a man called as Cody reached the door to his room.

"We can't pollute," he said, and didn't understand why they all laughed.

He'd waited so long to go to the bathroom that now it seemed to take forever. To pass the time, he stared at himself in the wall mirror. His reflection shocked him. Because he had always lived in a space cruiser, he'd never had the chance to get dirty. Now he hardly recognized himself—he was filthy! Dead leaves clung to his hair. His shorts and shirt were smudged and torn. In addition to the bleemie burns making big red blotches, his arms and legs were covered with scratches, scrapes, and muddy water trails.

He pulled off his ruined shirt and stuffed it into the waste disposal chute. The mirror showed big, ugly bruises over his ribs. Shorts followed shirt. Their removal revealed a large bruise on his hip. He remembered getting that when the skipper's foot hit him as he jumped into the bushes.

For some reason, thinking of that made him start to shake so badly that he had to sit down on the toilet to avoid falling. All the fear and pain he couldn't allow himself to feel during the day came back in a rush. He grabbed the towel, buried his face in it, and bit down on his hand to keep his cries from being overheard outside.

By the time he blew his nose and wiped his eyes, he felt better. The familiar act of brushing his teeth was calming; the water made him remember how thirsty he was, and he gulped down three cups full. The warm shower felt good until the soap hit his wounds. The bleemie spots burned so much that tears came to his eyes, but he had to use soap—the dirt wouldn't come off without it.

Minutes later, wearing clean shorts and a bathrobe, with his hair still wet, he was in Avi's room, stretched out on the table of a portable medcheck unit, being examined.

Avi seemed unusually quiet. Feeling guilty about not telling her the truth, Cody assumed that she had had time to remember that he had broken the rules.

"Will you get a reprimand because of this? Because I went out alone?"

"No." Avi didn't sound mad, just distracted.

"Will I get sent back to the ship?"

"No . . . Why? Do you want to be?"

"No! I just thought that . . . uh, if I'm a bother, that you might, uh, feel about me like my parents do. You might want someone else to be responsible for me."

That got Avi's full attention. "How long have you worried about this?"

"Always, I guess. Since I was old enough to understand."

Avi didn't say anything for so long that Cody was sure he was in deep trouble. "Nothing you might do could make me stop being responsible for you, as you put it," she said finally. "You're stuck with me, so get used to the idea. Understand?"

"Yes." Cody was so relieved he sat up and hugged her.

"Both of your parents, by the way, were out looking for you. On foot. They do care about you."

Cody thought that over. "They probably thought it would look funny if they didn't," he said.

"Now don't make unfair assumptions about them. You—" Avi interrupted herself. "Where did you get those bruises?" Her firm hands turned the patient toward the bright light. "Like someone dug their fingers into your ribs . . . on both sides. And there on your legs . . ."

"Maybe when I fell on the rocks?"

"No . . . this looks like someone grabbed you . . . someone with long nails. Hold still—there's a cut." Startlingly cold healant stung against Cody's side, but before he could protest, Avi dabbed another cut, then looked him in the eye. "You didn't get those bruises by falling, Cody. And you didn't wander off and get lost. You'd never be that careless. Now tell me what really happened."

Cody met her eyes and hesitated, wanting to tell and yet afraid. For if he told her about the skippers, Avi might feel she had to tell the local authorities, and the skippers might be punished or even killed.

He considered sticking to his story of getting lost, of embroidering it to make it more believable, but he'd never been a good liar, and especially not to Avi. Telling a lie meant having to tell another, and remembering each one.

"I'm waiting."

"I know."

"Is it so bad you can't talk about it? Do you want anti-traum?"

"No. If I tell, promise you won't tell anyone else? It's not about people. Not human-type people."

Dr. Avichenko frowned at that. "Oh?" she said carefully. "All right. As your physician, I can't reveal anything you tell me in confidence. Unless you give me permission to do so." She went on with the exam, the machine beeping to itself as it recorded the data picked up by the hand scanner. "You've been hurt by someone. I want to know what happened. Please?"

". . . did you ever hear of *skippers?*"

"No." Avi shook her head. "Why?"

"They're animals—creatures—that live here."

"There are so many exotic things on new worlds that I quit trying to remember them all," she admitted. "Do they have anything to do with your being lost?"

"Yes," said Cody, and told her the story.

Chapter 11

He talked until three the next morning. Even eating a sandwich didn't slow him down. Once started, he couldn't stop. He thought, in his exhaustion, that if he told her *everything* she would understand and forgive the skippers for what they had done.

Avi was a good audience; she truly listened. She went from being angry and horrified at hearing how he was captured and carried out to sea, to murmuring, "Poor things—they must have been so frightened, so confused," when he told about skippers being taken as specimens. She asked intent questions about their religion and the way they lived. But by two-thirty in the morning, she was visibly fighting sleep, worn out by the stress of the day.

"What do you think?" said Cody, when he finally finished and Avi didn't say anything for a minute or more.

"I think you're right. We shouldn't exact retribution." Seeing his puzzled look, she explained, "People shouldn't punish them. I think, too, that you're very brave. Most people would still be having hysterics after what you've been through. And I think we'd better get some sleep before we both pass out on the floor."

"But what do you think about the skippers?"

"Pretty much what you do. I agree that they should be our secret—at least until I have a chance to do some research. Now off to bed, and don't forget to code your door so the cleaning drone doesn't wake you."

He slept until hunger woke him at dinnertime the next day. Sitting up, groggy, he glanced down at his arms and gave a little moan of dismay at remembering everything. The bleemie burns had paled to an ugly pink rash. Scabs on his hands and knees hurt when he moved. The wet boots had left shiny blisters on both heels and three toes. Four fingernails were broken, several to the quick.

As he slowly took in all this damage, the thought occurred to him that life was a lot harder on a planet. A person got exposed to so many things that could never happen on a ship or even in a habitat. Unless he got into a really bad fight.

"You're a mess," he told his reflection in the sanit mirror. His hair was standing at odd angles, and his pillow had left a crease down one cheek.

By the time he could make himself presentable enough to go out into the lounge, everyone had gone to dinner. The entertainment screen was playing to an empty room—or so he thought until Dr. Palchek got up from a chair hidden behind a tubbed plant near the door. Cody smiled, and after a moment she returned the smile, almost shyly.

"How are you?" she asked.

"Fine, thank you."

"You look a bit the worse for wear."

"Just on the outside," said Cody, embarrassed by the remark. "Inside I'm fine. The medcheck said so."

"I'm sure she—it did." Dr. Palchek glanced at

the screen where two robot comics were exchanging noisy insults. "Ah, I had hoped to see you last night, but you were already in med-check by the time we got back from the field."

"Thank you for looking for me." Cody couldn't think of anything else to say. "Gus, too. I appreciate it."

"Yes, well, one never knows . . ." His mother seemed as unsure as Cody as to how to end this awkward meeting. "Uh, I'm meeting a friend at the hotel in town, but I wanted to give you this." Holding out a small box, she said, "Here," and tossed it across the space between them.

"Thank you." Cody caught the gift. "Don't you want to wait until I open it?"

Already halfway out the door, she paused in flight. "No . . . You'll enjoy it more alone, I think." She turned to regard him. "I should have made sure you had one long before this. I apologize." With that she went outside, and the door slid shut behind her.

Frowning to himself, Cody sat down and opened the box. Inside was an expensive chron-com with a gold wristband. The wearer could not only tell the time but talk with anyone wearing a similar unit within a surface range of one hundred miles—so the little booklet in the box informed him. The unit also contained an emergency button which, if pressed, would signal any passing satellite and tell it the wearer's location.

He put it on, admiring its gleaming bulk on his wrist. Some of the crew had chroncoms, but none as nice as this. If he'd had this yesterday, he could have called for help. Or pressed the emergency button. He wanted to press that button now, just to see what would happen, but he controlled the urge. He'd been in enough trouble.

His mother had said she should have given him one of these "long before." Did that mean she cared what happened to him? At least more than he had thought she cared?

By the time he ran outside, her rental car had already lifted off. There was no chance to tell her how much he liked her gift. Except to call her in flight—but he was too shy with her to do that.

As he crossed the lawn to the dining room, he wondered how Avi would react. She'd been fine about the camcorder, but this was something else.

Because he was the only child, Avi had explained, adults tended to give him almost anything he wanted. While they meant well, their generosity might give him unrealistic expectations of life outside the ship's society. "When you go to Earth to complete your education," Avi had warned, "you'll find that people your own age are commonplace. You won't be unique. Or special."

"There he is!" Emory yelled when Cody walked into the dining room. "Finally awake! Come in here, boy! Tell us where all you went yesterday while we went crazy hunting you."

Alerted by the cry, other people called to Cody, asking how he was, and in general making a satisfying fuss over him.

When he went to the autoserv, people on their way out of the room stopped to talk to him. By the time he was able to order, he was starving. He got two portions of fish and chips, a salad (because people nagged him if he didn't eat vegetables), pineapple pudding, and a slice of chocolate cake. Then he turned around to see who he should sit with.

The room had been crowded when he came in. Now only a few tables remained occupied. While he'd been talking, people had finished eating and left.

"Cody. Over here." Avi waved from a big table by the window. She sat alone, drinking coffee.

"I guess I slept pretty late," Cody said as he approached.

Avi looked at his loaded tray and smiled but made no comment—which Cody appreciated. Lately a lot of his friends had started to kid him about how much he could eat.

"I'm starved." He poked a crisp hot potato into his mouth and crunched. It was wonderful. "Want some?" He offered Avi his other plate of fish and chips.

"No thanks. I just finished eating."

"Oh yeah!" said Cody, remembering. "Look what Olivia gave me." He held out his left arm so that Avi could admire his gift while he explained how it worked. "Is it too expensive?"

"Probably," said Avi, "but it's beautiful."

"I can keep it?"

"Of course." She hesitated. "When I said what I did about expensive gifts, I didn't mean gifts from your parents. They should—" She corrected herself. "They can give you anything they want to."

"Gus never gives me anything." Cody's observation was just that, not a complaint or a judgment.

"Well, that's . . . Gus. It's nothing personal. Listen." Avi lowered her voice and changed the subject. "I spent most of the day researching skippers for you. Don't ask how I got the codes. Everything about them is classified. But if you want to see the files, you'll have to do it tonight. That was the only access time I could arrange."

"But what did you find out?" whispered Cody, impatient with this detail. "Do people know how smart they are? About the talking and the religion, all that stuff?"

"Religion isn't mentioned. You'll have to listen to the data. Then we can discuss it." Her eyes left his face and surveyed the room. "Sitting here whispering isn't the smartest way to avoid attracting attention." She looked back at him with a smile and said in a normal tone. "How's the fish?"

"Great," he said. "I may go get another helping."

Chapter 12

When he had heard and read the data, Cody understood all too well why it had been classified and kept secret. What he learned in those few hours—both about skippers *and* humans—made him very sad.

From the time of the first landing expedition, the corporation had been aware of the skippers' intelligence. Many studies had been done on the creatures, most far too advanced for Cody to understand.

An anthropologist had named them *skippers* after observing a dancelike ritual the creatures had performed for their alien visitors. The anthropologist's notes described them as "an aboriginal society of tribal hunter-gatherers, gentle, nonaggressive, much given to complex vocalizations." He noted "several immature specimens kept as pets quickly learned to mimic human speech."

A report done some years later, after a translator program had decoded their language, described them as having "complex speech patterns, rich in poetic imagery, similar to other primitive races in its lack of realism." That report also found them to be "highly superstitious," as well as "lacking any technology and thus unable to threaten, adapt to, or resist an advanced species."

The most recent file was an informal economic study entitled *Update: Development Costs Versus Native Population.* The study included financial details with figures so large that they had no real meaning to Cody. Especially since he had never had to pay for anything in his life. The report said the skipper population had "downsized from an original estimate of two million worldwide to less than two hundred thousand . . . and appears to have stabilized there."

The report concluded: "Should the native population in any way impede development, it can, at minimal cost, be confined to remote reservation areas and be disposed of by seemingly natural causes, such as induced Yeltzin's disease."

Cody played that sentence back twice to be sure he understood, not wanting to believe it. He never thought humans would do something that cruel, especially to helpless creatures.

The skippers were doomed. No matter what they did, no matter what they truly were, they were going to die. And how had they gone from two million to a tenth of that? *By seemingly natural causes?*

"Can I make copies of this?" he asked, turning to Avi.

"Absolutely not!" Seeing that Cody was going to argue the point, she explained, "I can't tell you how I got access to these files, but I'm sure copying them would set off alarms. Besides, what would you do with them? Confront an exec? Put both our lives in jeopardy?"

"You mean—we might be killed for knowing this?" Cody found that hard to believe, but Avi never lied to him.

She hesitated before answering. "I suspect that is a possibility."

Cody shivered as the full meaning of the

threat became clear. "But they're going to kill the skippers!" He was so angry at the unfairness of it that he was close to tears. "Or make them die, and that's the same thing. It's against Federation law. Even *I* know that!"

"And there is absolutely nothing we can do about it." Avi reached over and touched the console, sending the data back to File for safekeeping. "And lower your voice. I'm not sure how soundproof these rooms are."

"They can't get away with this just because nobody pays attention. They can't," said Cody, lowering his voice. "It's not fair! It's so wrong! Humans shouldn't even be on this planet. Why are we? Just for money? I'm going—"

"Cody Oakton! Listen to me!" Avi firmly cradled his face in her hands, both to calm him and to get his full attention. "Listen!" she repeated. "We can't do anything about it! Don't interrupt! I debated letting you know all this. I decided you should know, not because you need an education in how rotten people can be but to keep you from getting into serious trouble.

"This data represents the official corporate policy where Patma is concerned. That policy won't change. There are very few planets where life exists. There are even fewer where *human* life can exist. The time and cost involved to locate and develop these Earth-type planets is enormous. So enormous that Federation laws governing new planets might be ignored. Money is very powerful. Trillions were spent to discover Patma. To develop it to its present crude state cost more trillions. At this point, no corporation would forfeit its investment because of what they consider a few primitive native inhabitants."

Cody interrupted. "You're saying that if we find a planet where humans can live, we just move in and take it! Even if intelligent aliens already live there?"

"I don't know of any other world where our corporation has done that, but then I didn't know about the skippers," admitted Avi. "Not that custom excuses the practice, but it is nothing new. I've heard that a planet in the Eridani system was inhabited by city-building sentients when Tri-Mak's ship arrived there. Their next ship carried archaeologists to study Tri-Mak's ruins.

"When you go to Earth and study our ancient history, you'll see the pattern repeated in one civilization after another, over thousands of years. People with superior technology or numbers move in, take over, and destroy the people who were there first. Europeans destroyed the native Americans. . . ."

Seeing that these names meant nothing to the boy, Avi paused. "*Might makes right* is a fact of life, I'm afraid," she concluded sadly. "You can't change it, and you're in no position to try.

"Until you go to Earth to finish your education, you're a guest on the *Annie Cannon.* Not an employee. You have no contract, no real legal rights. You live in the corporation's ship—and in its worlds—because it allows you to. If you create problems for the corporation out here, it can—and probably will—create bigger problems for you. And your parents, and probably for me, too."

"Like what?" Cody asked, feeling very depressed.

Avi shook her head. "I don't know. And I hope I don't find out."

The crash of the surf at high tide could be heard in the silence of the room as Avi let him think things over. From somewhere outside the window, a night creature sang a soft trilling song, interrupted at intervals by a series of clicks.

"If I tell them how I met the skippers in the first place, they'll kill them for running away with me, won't they?" Cody said at last. He sounded tired.

"I don't know," said Avi, "but if you liked the

skippers, keep quiet about them. Let them live in peace while they can."

After another long silence, Cody let out a big sigh. "I promise, whatever I do, that it won't be anything that gets you or the skippers or anyone else in trouble. So don't worry about it."

"I'm sorry, Cody, for disillusioning you about people. I wish none of this had happened. But it has, and I can't see any way to change that."

She looked so miserable that he got up and gave her an impulsive hug. "I know," he said. "If I hadn't gone to the beach alone, none of this would have happened. Neither of us would know anything about skippers . . . and I wouldn't have learned all this other stuff. . . ."

He fell silent at that, thinking that it wasn't the big things that changed your life but the little ones. Things you never expected to have any consequences. Coming to the planet's surface was a big thing, but nothing really changed until he went to the beach, a little nothing thing.

He'd already decided he was going to save the skippers—or at least try. He lay awake half the night trying to think of a way to do that.

The big skipper said they believed "each one thing" was important, that one affected all, that each animal or plant or person could change the world by being or not being, doing or not doing.

If that were true, and he believed it was, maybe he was that one person who would make a difference to them? Maybe that was why he was the only child born on the *Annie Cannon.*

By the time he fell asleep, he had devised a plan. He would make a record of what the skippers really were, and when he went to Earth to go to college, he would take that record with him. When he had learned how, he would submit it to the Federation Court. Once the judges understood the situation, he was sure the court would demand the skippers be protected.

If that didn't work, then he would find a way to tell Earth's people about what was happening here on Patma. Maybe they'd quit buying things exported from the planet. Maybe no one would want to come here if they knew what the corporation was doing to keep this planet. They couldn't develop the world without people. In fact, he thought, maybe he would tell people first. It might be safer that way.

Only twenty days remained of the crew's surface leave, but that should be time enough. The biggest problem would be going back to the sacred cave with the camcorder and then getting back to the hotel without being found out.

It would be dangerous. The skippers might want to hold him hostage again. That was scary.

He might be seen and stopped by Patma security. If recorded proof of the skipper's intelligence was taken from him by local authorities, they might destroy not only his camcorder but the cave—and maybe the skippers, too. That would be a terrible way for him to *matter.*

And then there was Avi to consider. And Olivia and Gus . . .

He turned and twisted in his bed and felt sick to his stomach. Maybe he should forget the whole idea? Maybe wanting to save the skippers was just a way for him to feel important? Maybe he wasn't meant to matter. Maybe being here, even being born, was all an accident?

His sleep was restless. Bad dreams made him moan and cry out so loudly that Avi overheard him in the next room. She came in to see what was wrong. When Cody muttered "skippers" in answer to her whispered concern, she told him, "It's just a dream. You'll never see them again."

CHAPTER 13

For the next week, Cody had no time to himself. Half the crew wanted to take him on field trips. He suspected Avi had asked them to keep him busy, so he wouldn't get in more trouble.

She denied that, explaining, "It's a normal thing. The crew's had a chance to rest, and now they're ready to go sightseeing. They want you to go along because they like you. And you should go. It'll be educational. Take your camcorder."

Cody had no good excuse for refusing, so he went. He enjoyed most of the trips. At times the attention he attracted made him self-conscious. People stared, a few made tasteless jokes about "kids," but most seemed glad to see him. He was told repeatedly, "You remind me of my son" or "my kid brother" or someone else left behind.

He was flown down the coast to a logging operation where machines were clear-cutting a tall forest. The next day Emory took him to a gem mine and after that to the factory in town where the gems were cut and polished. In days to follow he toured experimental farms and chemical plants, seashell warehouses and new apartment buildings. Everything was interesting, but it was not what he really wanted to be doing.

Just when he started to despair of ever being left alone again, the crew of another ship arrived on leave. There was a party. Unplanned, it began in midafternoon in the dining room bar. Old friendships were renewed and celebrated. By the time Cody went in for dinner, the room was loud with talk and laughter.

He looked around and grinned to himself. Maybe things would work out after all. Almost everyone was drinking. If this party was like the big parties on the ship—and since nobody had to worry about going on duty tomorrow—he just might be the only person awake in the morning.

He got his dinner from the autoserv, then chose a table away from the crowd, where he could watch the room while he ate. Yes! There definitely was reason to hope that tomorrow he could go see the skippers! His friends would not be waking up early.

By the time he finished eating, an impromptu band had started to play. People were dancing.

A few people came over to talk to him, but most either waved hello or didn't notice him at all. Parties like this always made him uncomfortably aware of being the only child among adults. He went to bed earlier than usual, glad that the chance he had hoped for had come but sorry to be excluded from the fun.

A noise woke him before dawn. The outside lights revealed a man sleeping in the flower bed under his window, mouth open, snoring loudly. With each snore, a red flower bending over the man's face waved in the air flow. Cody watched the flower waving, then went and got his camcorder and filmed the scene.

The stars were still visible. Far out over the ocean, a cloud bank was turning a faint pink with morning. He decided to get dressed and go.

To his surprise, now that the time had come, the thought of actually going back there was so scary he wasn't sure he could do it. Remembering his terror as the skippers chased him over the beach that night made him so queasy that he had to sit back down on his bed to deep-breathe and regain his courage.

He decided the only way for his plan to work was to find the big skipper before landing. He had to—the big skipper was the only one who could understand what he wanted to do . . . and the only one he trusted not to kill him.

Remembering the bleemies and their acid burns, he put on a long-sleeved, hooded jumpsuit and surface shoes that were like sturdy sneakers. Wearing his chroncom gave him confidence; he could call for help if he had to. Helmet and camcorder went into his backpack, along with a handful of blank recordets. After a moment's thought, he added another handful, just in case.

He opened his door to see if anybody was up to see him go. The lounge was deserted. He left Avi a note saying that he'd gone out to photograph animals and would be back after lunch and not to worry.

A cleaner drone was vacuuming the floor of the empty dining room. Cody ordered scrambled eggs and a sweet roll. While his breakfast heated, he went to the take-out server and got two mung buns, a pack of cookies, and four ice-tubes to add to his backpack. The icetubes would cool the food and serve as drinking water. He ate hurriedly, put on his helmet, and went out to the yard where the air scooters were kept.

The rental screen showed no scooters had been checked out yet, which meant no one else was up. Cody chose a new one, tan with a red seat.

The outside lighting was still on, but when Cody's scooter rose above the cabana roof, he saw that the pink streak along the horizon had turned orange. The waves sparkled with reflected light.

It was the first dawn he'd ever seen. Its beauty awed him. From a starship, one could never imagine this effect of a sun on one of its planets. He recorded the sunrise with his camcorder.

It was fun being out this early, flying along in the morning breeze. The growing light revealed a variety of seabirds and animals below him, feeding along the beach. Some of the larger animals looked up, not sure if they should run. Black against the morning sky, enormous flocks of birds flew out over the ocean from somewhere inland. He decided they slept in the thickets and were going out for breakfast.

Flying low over the cliffs, Cody thought he recognized those he had climbed in the dark. Any tracks left behind were gone, washed away or erased by blowing sand.

He was shocked when, in less than twenty minutes, the offshore rock formation of the four crouching animals came into view. He had to remind himself that the scooter flew much faster than he could walk or the skippers could swim.

In the distance, skippers were out swimming. By the time he was close enough to see if the honey-colored one was there, they had fled the water and were running toward the thicket. The sound of their voices calling to one another came up on the breeze, loud enough to be heard over the sound of the scooter.

From the air, the thicket canopy hid any sign of the busy life below. Unless one had seen the caves and pathways, there was no way of knowing they existed. Cody circled until the river in which he had washed his bleemie burns came into view. Then he flew upstream until he could see the little beach below the caves.

There was movement beneath the leaf canopy—more skippers running away. Seeing how afraid they were gave him added confidence in spite of his own fear. What didn't occur to him was that their fear made them more dangerous.

"Hello?" he called, circling lower until the breeze of the scooter's passing rustled the leaves. "Hello? Are you down there, Mr. Skipper?"

There was no answer.

Trying to see through the thicket and fly at the same time was a problem. He pulled the scooter up to clear the hillside and circled again.

"Hello? It's me, Cody. I have to talk to you."

Finally, when he had almost decided he would have to give up and go back to the hotel defeated, he heard the honey-colored skipper answer.

"Go away!" it called.

Chapter 14

The heavy smell of leaves, mud, and water rose to meet Cody as he landed on the sandbar. "I'm down here," he called, shutting off the power.

There was no answer. He could hear the river running over the stones and gravel. In the distance a bird or insect said *tsk-tsk-tsk* over and over. He looked all around. No skippers were in sight, but he knew they had to be watching him. It was too quiet.

When he had landed, Cody decided to leave the scooter here in the open and walk up to meet the honey-colored skipper at the caves. The longer he sat listening to this watchful silence, the less that seemed like a good idea. He might need to escape *fast.* He turned the power on again.

"Hello? I know you're up there. Can I come up?"

"Go away!"

"We have to talk. I want to help you."

"Go away!"

It sounded as if the skipper was standing near the door to the big cave, right at the top of the path.

Cody thought it over. A smart person would give up and go back to the hotel. But if he gave up now, for the rest of his life he'd remember that maybe he could have helped the skippers and didn't.

"So you're not a smart person," he told himself.

Before entering the path, Cody pictured in his mind how he could escape, if he had to. *Fly up to the cave. If the big skipper isn't there, go full power, up through the leaf canopy and out and away!* He was counting on the other skippers to be too scared of the scooter to get near him.

Going up the tunnellike path was slow, more like floating than flying. He had to keep the scooter about a foot above the ground. Any higher and the rollbars brushed the leaves and knocked off bleemies. Any lower and he scraped bottom. The farther he went, the more nervous he became.

Halfway up, two big brown skippers came charging out of the bushes, blocking his way. Startled, Cody swerved wildly. Branches snapped against the scooter cage. The unit nearly tipped over before he regained control and managed to back away.

"You nearly made me wreck!" he yelled in anger, not thinking. He had forgotten how big they were, and how strange looking.

The skippers came after him. One struck at him through the bars. He dodged the claws, but the other skipper gripped a rollbar and pushed the scooter firmly into the sand.

"Stop it! You'll bend the frame!" Noise behind him made him turn around. More skippers were pushing their way through the bushes. He was surrounded. "Get away! Let me go!"

He pressed the Lift button so hard his finger hurt, wanting the scooter to go straight up through the branches. Who cared about bleemies! He wanted out of here! But pressing the Lift button only made him bounce up and down as the skippers held the scooter.

From somewhere ahead a voice shouted. It sounded like the honey-colored skipper, but he couldn't be sure. The eyestalks of the skippers threatening him raised and swiveled. The skipper holding the front bars muttered something to the one next to him, but neither moved.

There was movement behind the pair as skippers pressed back into the bushes to clear the path. To his great relief Cody saw *his* skipper approaching. He took his finger off the Lift button. The scooter quit bouncing.

Without warning, the big skipper gave a roar of anger, reared up on its back legs, front and midlegs waving, mouth open, teeth exposed. Its brown belly was as shiny as a segmented shield.

Cody stared up. The thing seemed twelve feet tall. Suddenly he was sure he was about to be squashed, scooter and all.

If he was scared, so were his attackers. They instantly backed away into the bushes—although he didn't notice until later that they had gone.

After scanning the area, the big creature slowly lowered itself to the ground. In the quiet, Cody heard its body creak. The skipper stood looking down at him.

Wind rustled the leaves around them and

Cody shivered. His mouth felt paper-dry. He tried licking his lips but had no saliva. "Wha—" He cleared his throat. "What did you say to them?" He forced out the words to end the threatening silence.

The skipper took its own good time answering. "I reminded them that you were young, lacking an adult's mind," it said finally. It didn't sound friendly. "Why else would you come back here? You put yourself in danger. You are a danger to us. Go away! Now!"

"No! I have a plan to help you. Now that I'm here, I'm not leaving until you listen to me."

"For all of your kind to leave is the only way to help this world."

"That's true," Cody agreed. "And maybe we can make them go if you'll just listen. You're wasting time by arguing. I thought *you'd* understand."

For an instant the skipper's stalked eyes looked up to the sky in a manner suggesting almost human exasperation. "Do you know what . . . who you are speaking to?"

"Aren't you the leader here?" said Cody.

"I am. I am also . . . I do not know your word . . . and you will not know ours. I am the . . . oldest, most respected of all our people. *All* our people."

"Leader," Cody repeated, glad to know he

was dealing with the highest authority. "*Leader* is our word. And I do respect you. But I don't have much time. Please, let me tell—"

"No! You can only put us in danger . . . bring other humans here to destroy us. Bring—"

"If I wanted to do that, they would have been here the next morning!" Nerves, not rudeness, made Cody interrupt. "You told me each one thing is special, that one affects all the rest. If you truly believe that, then even though I'm human, I have to matter to you. And you have to listen to me."

One of the skipper's amber eyes searched Cody's face as if looking for meaning there. The other big eye, like a scanning device, surveyed the gathering crowd. Lids closed over the small eyes. "Come," it said finally. "In your machine." It turned and started up the hill.

The other skippers whispered among themselves as Cody followed their leader. All the way up the path Cody was afraid of bumping into his host's legs and knocking him down. If that happened, he thought the others would kill him. When he finally entered the dim antechamber to the Sacred Caves, he gave a big sigh of relief, turned off the scooter, and took off his helmet.

After assigning a guard at the entrance, the

skipper turned to him. "Yess," it hissed. "You do well to remind me. You matter, young human. I may not understand why, but there is a reason you came to this world." It paused. "So I believe. You have reason to fear us, yet you came back. I will listen to you."

Cody thought the skipper might not understand about corporations and money. Since he didn't understand such things himself, he decided to omit that part. The skippers probably knew better than he did how many of their kind had died since humans came to their world, so he didn't want to talk about that either, or about the corporation's plans for the skippers' future.

Instead he began by telling the skipper about the laws of the Federation of Worlds. Those laws said that when a world was inhabited by intelligent beings, other intelligent beings were supposed to leave them alone. "But because they want this world for themselves, our people haven't told anyone that you skippers are intelligent. So I intend to try to do that. I can't promise I'll succeed, but I'm going to try."

Cody explained that he would be going to Earth to be educated. That was why he wanted to take with him proof of the skippers' right to their own planet. He showed the skipper how the camcorder worked. He demonstrated how recordet cards could—by touching the colored dots—hear, retain, and repeat all their myths and stories or anything else the skippers wanted the Federation Court to know about them.

"But I only have time to record the Sacred Caves on the camcorder and get pictures of you and as many of your people as I can. I have to get back to the hotel before anyone starts looking for me. They think I was lost before. Only one person knows what really happened—and she won't ever tell. But I don't want anyone, not even her, to know I came here again."

When Cody was finally through talking, the skipper said thoughtfully, "You plan to betray your own kind. If you are able to bring our cause before your judges, will you be sorry you did this when you are an adult?"

"No . . ." Cody hadn't thought of that possibility. "I don't think so. What my people are doing here is wrong, and against the law. And it will always be wrong."

The skipper made a hissing noise. "We are so sure of things when we are young. Do you know, if you succeed, what will happen to your people here? Where they will go? How they will live? Will they suffer?"

"There are other worlds for them. Or they can go back to where they came from."

"And they can live there?" the skipper asked.

"Yes." Cody thought the skipper wouldn't be so worried about what might happen to Patma's humans if it knew what some of them planned to do to skippers.

"You are sure they can do this?" the skipper said.

"Yes! How do you think they found this world?"

The skipper regarded him for a time, then said, "Your machine will be safe here while we are in the Sacred Caves."

Chapter 15

By midmorning, Cody had everything he needed.

Every part of the caves had been photographed. He had recorded the skipper's explanation of how and why the Sacred Caves existed. He had pictures of skippers of all ages, their cavelike homes, and their garden plots hidden along the river.

Cody left the recordet cards with the skipper and showed it which button to press to record and which to play back. The skipper had promised to fill them with their myths and history—"As well as I can. Our words are . . . not like yours." Then the cards were to be taken by night to Cody's little cave on the beach. That seemed to Cody a fitting ending.

"I probably won't ever see you again," Cody said as he rolled the scooter out of the cave. The thought made him sad.

"No," agreed the skipper. "Your kind, I think, does not live as long as ours."

That answer shocked Cody into silence for a moment. Self-absorbed, he'd given little thought to the fact that this skipper was *young* when humans first came to Patma. By human time it was almost three hundred years old. With luck it might live to see humans leave its world.

"What I meant was," Cody said slowly, "if the Federation Court makes the corporation leave Patma, humans won't be allowed to come here any more. I can't come back."

"If the humans leave," said the skipper, "you will become part of our sacred history. Your image will be carved in a special place in our caves. From this day on, we will speak of you always in our prayers. Do you have a name?"

"Cody." He considered telling the skipper his

last name, but that was Gus's name, too. "Just Cody."

"You will be in our prayers, Just Cody."

The idea of being remembered in the prayers of aliens light-years away was touching, and somehow comforting. So far as he knew, no one had ever said a prayer for him. "Thank you," he said. "I like that." He had to swallow before he could go on. "But since it will take so long for me to get to Earth . . . By the time you know if I succeeded, how will you remember what I looked like?"

"We will remember," the skipper assured him. It held out one of the recordets. "Take this and speak yourself into it. Put it in your cave to be picked up. Then I will have the voice of the one friend to come to our world from the stars. The one who mattered."

Cody's last view of the skippers was of eyes and antennae raised skyward as the scooter rose up through an opening in the thicket canopy. He flew over the path leading to the beach and turned left.

Halfway back to the hotel, he landed to take the disc out of the camcorder and put it safely in his pocket. Inserting a fresh disc, he recorded the ocean. Then, setting the camcorder on a rock, he recorded himself walking along the shore.

If anybody asked what he had recorded that morning, he wanted to have something to show for his time. And he wanted to remember how he looked and felt today. Not that he was never happy, but today he was *aware* of being happy for the first time in his life. And he couldn't stop smiling.

While he'd always wanted to be an adult, equal and independent, part of him had always dreaded growing up. To grow up meant going to Earth, leaving behind not only Avi and Emory but everything and everyone familiar. And while adults told him they had all done that, he felt it wasn't quite the same for them.

Now he looked forward to it all. He was going to matter. And he had the next four years, during the voyage to Earth, to decide if he wanted to study law, if that could help the skippers and other creatures like them.

A white-and-brown seabird landed on the roll-bar above his head and peered down at him with liquid black eyes. When the scooter lifted off, the bird croaked a cry but rode along until the hotel came into view. Cody was sorry when it flew away.

Although it was almost noon, the swimming pools were deserted. So was the courtyard. His note to Avi was still halfway under her door. He retrieved the note, still smiling, and went into his room to put away his backpack and camcorder.

He hid the very special disc among all his other discs; he would find a safer place for it later, in his room on the *Annie Cannon.*

"Hey, Little Bit," Emory called through the open door. "You feel like going for a ride with me? Or have you been out already?"

"Yes," said Cody. "Both. But I want to see all of this world I can, in case I never get to come back."

Emory grinned at him, misunderstanding Cody's smile. "For a basically sad thought," the man said, "it sure seems to make you happy."